Glitter Beach

Special thanks to Linda Chapman

To Sarah Hawkins, for making the
Secret Kingdom the magical,
wonderful place it is!

ISBN 978-0-545-53558-8

12 11 10 9 8 7 6 5 4 3 2 1   15 16 17 18 19 20/0

Printed in the U.S.A.   40
First Scholastic printing, February 2015

Secret Kingdom

Glitter Beach

ROSIE BANKS

Scholastic Inc.

Contents

The Adventure Begins

"Hi, Mom! I'm home!"

Ellie Macdonald ran into the empty kitchen through the back door. She shrugged her schoolbag off her shoulders and put it down carefully. After all, there was something very special inside! At the bottom, wrapped up in her school sweater, was a mysterious wooden box.

As she opened her bag, Ellie felt a flicker of excitement. She and her best friends, Summer Hammond and Jasmine Smith, were the only ones who knew that the box was much more than an ordinary jewelry box. It had been made by the ruler of a magical land called the Secret Kingdom, where incredible creatures like fairies, mermaids, unicorns, and pixies lived. It was a wonderful place, but it was in terrible trouble.

When everyone in the land had decided they wanted kind King Merry to rule rather than his horrid sister, Queen Malice, the evil queen had sent six thunderbolts crashing into different parts of the kingdom. Each thunderbolt had the power to make trouble and bring great unhappiness. Ellie and her friends

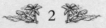

had promised to help stop the nasty queen. Whenever one of her thunderbolts caused a problem in the Secret Kingdom, a riddle would appear in the lid of the Magic Box to tell the girls where they were needed. When they solved it, Ellie, Summer, and Jasmine would be whisked away to the kingdom to try to help. They had already had five wonderful adventures and Ellie couldn't wait for the magic to work again!

Ellie pulled the Magic Box out of her bag and looked hopefully at the carvings of amazing creatures that covered every side and the glittering jewels that decorated its mirrored lid. If only the lid would start glowing, that would mean it was time for her and her friends to return to the Secret Kingdom. But all she could

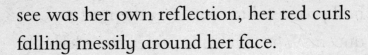

see was her own reflection, her red curls
falling messily around her face.

Ellie sighed and carefully carried the
box to the hall. She caught sight of her
mom through the window, tidying up the
hanging baskets in the front garden. Ellie
avoided her and headed for the stairs,
clutching the Magic Box.

"RARRRRR!" With a loud yell, Molly, Ellie's little sister, jumped out from where she had been hiding beside the hall table.

Ellie almost dropped the box in shock. "Molly!"

Molly whooped in delight. "I made you jump, Ellie!" She was four and looked just like Ellie had when she was little, with red curls that reached her shoulders and mischievous green eyes. She loved to play tricks on her big sister. "What's that?" she said curiously, spotting the box in Ellie's arms.

"Nothing."

"Let me see!" Molly tried to look.

"It's just an old box, Mol," Ellie told her hastily. The last thing she wanted was Molly looking in the Magic Box! Inside

it were six wooden compartments, and five of them were filled with the special objects Ellie and the others had collected on their adventures. There was a magic moving map of the Secret Kingdom, a tiny silver unicorn horn that let the person holding it talk to animals, a crystal that could be used to control the weather, a pearl that could turn you invisible, and an icy hourglass that could be used to freeze time. If Molly found those things she'd want to know where they had come from, and the girls couldn't tell anyone about the Secret Kingdom!

Ellie swooped the box over her sister's head and put it on the table. Then, jumping forward, she started to tickle Molly to distract her.

Molly squealed and pushed her away. "Ellie, get off!"

Ellie tickled her harder. "Nope! I'm the tickle monster and I'm coming to get you!" she teased, chasing her around the hall.

Molly laughed and shrieked. "Get off me! Get off . . . *hic*!" A loud hiccup exploded from her and both sisters burst out laughing.

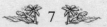

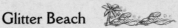

The front door opened. Mrs. Macdonald looked in. "What's going on, girls?"

Molly could barely contain her giggles. "Ellie was tickling me, Mommy, and now I've got . . . I've got . . . *Hic*!"

"Hiccups," Ellie finished for her with a grin.

"Oh, Molly." Mrs. Macdonald shook her head. "Come on, let's get you some water. Did you have a good day at school, Ellie?" she called over her shoulder as she led Molly away.

"Yes, fine, thanks, Mom. I'm just going up to my room for a while."

Grabbing the Magic Box, Ellie ran upstairs. After putting the box safely on her desk and changing out of her school clothes, she got out her sketchbook and began to draw a picture of Trixi, the little

royal pixie who the girls had met on all
their adventures. Ellie was very good at
art, but she still couldn't make the pixie
look as lively and friendly as she was in
real life.

Taking a rest for the moment, she
glanced up at the box and almost fell off
her chair in surprise.

It was glowing.

Ellie gasped and jumped to her feet,
sending her pencil
cup flying. "Oh
wow! It's time
for another
adventure!"

She threw
her school
sweater over
the box in case

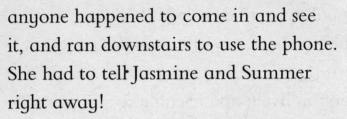

anyone happened to come in and see
it, and ran downstairs to use the phone.
She had to tell Jasmine and Summer
right away!

"Promise you won't look at the riddle
on the box until we get there!" begged
Jasmine when Ellie called her.

"I promise!" Ellie said, although she
was desperate to find out what the riddle
would say and where in the Secret
Kingdom they were needed this time.

Ellie waited impatiently by the front
door. Jasmine and Summer both lived in
Honeyvale, too, but it seemed to take
them ages to arrive. Each minute felt
like an hour! At last, she saw Summer
running along the street, her blond braids
flying out behind her. At the same time,

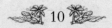

Jasmine came racing around the corner on her bike.

"It's really happening, then?" Jasmine breathed, pulling off her bike helmet, her dark hair tumbling around her shoulders.

"Yes!" Ellie said, happiness fizzing through her.

They hurried inside. "Hi, girls," Mrs. Macdonald called from the kitchen. "Are you staying for a snack?"

"Yes, please," Summer and Jasmine chorused.

"Though, hopefully, we'll have had an amazing adventure before then!" Jasmine whispered to Ellie and Summer. The girls knew that time in the real world stood still when they were in the Secret Kingdom, so Ellie's mom would never

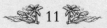

even notice that they'd been gone. They shared a smile and raced upstairs.

"Ta-da!" Ellie whisked her sweater off the box.

"Look!" Summer squealed. "We're really going to the Secret Kingdom again!"

"Who do you think we'll meet this time?" said Jasmine.

"Let's see what the riddle says!" Ellie carefully read out the words that had formed in the mirror:

> "Danger from a royal hand,
> A thunderbolt in sparkling sand,
> A wicked deed must be put right,
> Before the next midsummer night."

The girls looked at one another in confusion. "What does that mean?" said

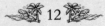

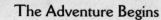

Summer, twiddling the end of one of her braids. "Where do we have to go?"

Suddenly the box opened and a piece of parchment floated out of it. It was the magic map!

Ellie carefully unfolded it, with Summer and Jasmine peering over her shoulders. The map glowed with color. Magical pictures on it showed what was happening on the crescent-shaped island of the Secret Kingdom, with its

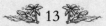

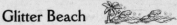

emerald-green hills and meadows,
aquamarine waters, and sandy coves.

"Look! There's Unicorn Valley!" said
Summer, looking down to where unicorns
were cantering far below, their silver and
gold horns glittering in the sunshine.

"And Magic Mountain," said Jasmine,
pointing to a huge snow-covered
mountain that had pixies all over it,
skiing and zooming down enormous
slides made of ice.

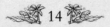

"I wonder where we're needed this time," said Ellie, her forehead crinkling in thought as she looked at the riddle again.

"It says 'a thunderbolt in sparkling sand'," said Summer. "Well, you get sand at the seaside — so maybe we have to go to a beach?"

"Glitter Beach!" gasped Jasmine, pointing to a label next to a little harbor with shops and boats. "Somewhere with a name like that is bound to have sparkling sand."

Ellie and Summer nodded eagerly.

Jasmine's hazel eyes shone in excitement. "What are we waiting for? Let's call Trixi!"

The girls put their hands on the green gems of the box and looked at one another. "The answer to the riddle is Glitter Beach!" they said together.

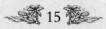

A Fairy Festival

There was a flash of light, and the drawings on Ellie's bedroom walls fluttered. The light was so bright that Ellie, Jasmine, and Summer all blinked. As their eyes flew open they heard a tinkling laugh. A familiar little pixie was hovering in front of them on a floating leaf!

"Trixibelle!" cried Jasmine happily. "You've come to take us on another adventure!"

"Hello, girls. It's lovely to see you again!" Trixi smiled.

"You look pretty!" Ellie said, looking at her pixie friend, who was wearing a bright yellow dress made out of sunflower petals and a pair of pretty sunglasses. A garland of multicolored flowers hung around her neck.

"I was just getting ready to go on a vacation!" Trixi flew a loop-the-loop on her leaf. "I'm so excited about it! My fairy friend, Willow, has invited me to

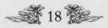

go to a special ceremony with her. All the fairies in the kingdom meet up every Midsummer's Eve to watch the kingdom's magic being renewed — and I'm going, too!"

Her words reminded Ellie of the Magic Box. "Oh!" she exclaimed. "The riddle said something about midsummer."

Trixi stopped twirling. "Goodness! I was so excited about my vacation I forgot that I normally only see you when something's gone wrong! Where did the Magic Box say the next thunderbolt is?"

"A place with sparkling sand," Ellie told her. "We think that might mean Glitter Beach."

Trixi read the riddle in the mirror on the Magic Box, and her blue eyes widened. "But that's where all the fairies

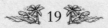

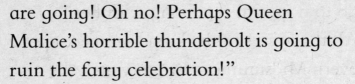

are going! Oh no! Perhaps Queen
Malice's horrible thunderbolt is going to
ruin the fairy celebration!"

"Don't worry," Ellie said quickly, seeing
the pixie's alarmed expression. "We'll
come with you to Glitter Beach. If a
thunderbolt has landed there, we'll fix
things!"

"Oh, thank you!" Trixi said gratefully.
She tapped her magic ring and chanted:

> *"The evil queen has trouble planned.*
> *Brave helpers fly to save our land!"*

As she spoke, the thunderbolt
riddle faded and her words formed
in the mirror. Ellie's purple bedroom
walls disappeared and the girls were
surrounded by shards of sunlight. Jasmine,

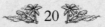

Ellie, and Summer grabbed one another's hands just in time as the magic whirled them away!

Around and around they turned until the magic set them down gently. There was the feel of sunshine on their skin and a gentle rocking under their feet.

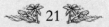

"Wow!" Ellie breathed as she opened her eyes. They were standing in a boat made out of a large white shell, which was being pulled by two huge silver dolphins. The aquamarine water splashed over their backs as they plunged through the waves, leaving a trail of snowy foam behind them. The sun shone down brightly from the forget-me-not-blue sky as they headed toward a small harbor with a shimmering beach.

"We're tiny!" Ellie realized suddenly as she saw that she was the same height as Trixi.

The others both gasped.

"That's why the dolphins look so big!" said Summer.

"I thought I had better make you small or you wouldn't be able to enjoy Glitter Beach properly. There's lots to see and do but it's all built for fairies!" Trixi explained.

"It's just amazing being this small," said Summer, throwing her arms

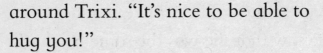

around Trixi. "It's nice to be able to hug you!"

Ellie put her hand to the top of her head to check for the tiara that always appeared when she went to the Secret Kingdom, to show that she was an important friend and helper of King Merry. Sure enough, it was there, reduced to teeny, tiny size just as Ellie was. Jasmine and Summer were wearing theirs, too.

"Glitter Beach is just ahead." Trixi waved an arm toward the harbor. The girls could just see pretty little shops and market stalls along the bay, and multicolored boats tied to the pier.

"Look, the boats have got wings instead of sails!" Jasmine called out as they got closer.

Trixi managed to smile. "That's because

those are fairy yachts. They fly as well as
sail in the water!"

"And look at the surfers!" exclaimed
Ellie.

All around them, fairies were surfing
on long, flat mussel shells. Dressed in
colorful bikinis or swimming trunks,
they raced across the waves, some
balancing with their arms out, others
spinning around or flying up into the
air before landing back on their boards,
their wings shimmering in the sunlight.

One was even doing a handstand on his board, keeping his balance by moving his wings delicately. He came zooming past the girls, sending a wave splashing all over them. They squealed.

"Sorry!" he called.

"We don't mind!" called Ellie, splashing him back.

"Oh, this is amazing!" said Jasmine, pushing back her long, dark hair.

"This is one of my favorite places in the whole kingdom," Trixi said. "And it's so important. At twelve o'clock every Midsummer's Eve, the golden sand turns to glitter dust for one minute. In that time, all the magic is returned to the land for another year. The fairies always come to watch it happen, but I've never seen it before — I can't wait!" Trixi looked down at her pixie ring. "I've had to do so many spells for King Merry this year that my magic's nearly all used up! Without the sand at Glitter Beach there would be no magic anywhere in the Secret Kingdom."

"Oh wow!" breathed Ellie. "Can *we* watch it happen?"

"Of course," replied Trixi.

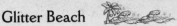

Summer had a thought. "Will . . . will the glitter dust give us magic, too?"

Trixi's forehead wrinkled. "I don't know. But tonight is an extra-magical night. Anything could happen!"

"Even if we could only do magic for a little while, it would be great!" said Jasmine, giving the others an excited look.

"We can't forget about Queen Malice's thunderbolt though," Summer warned. "Remember, we have to find it before it causes trouble."

Ellie and Jasmine nodded. They really did have to watch out! There was no telling what horrible things Queen Malice might have planned.

The dolphins pulled up to the wooden pier and the girls climbed out of the

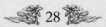

shell boat. Raising their heads out of the
water, the dolphins opened their mouths
in toothy grins.
Summer reached
up on tiptoe
and patted one
on the nose.
"Thank you
for the lift!"
she cried happily.

The dolphins
made a clicking noise that sounded like
"you're welcome!"

As Trixi flew her leaf out of the boat
another fairy rushed over and hugged
her. She was wearing a bright blue dress
with a red flower at the shoulder. Her
delicate wings were as aquamarine as the
sea, and she had wildflowers in her hair.

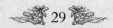

"Hello!" she said delightedly.

"Ellie, Summer, and Jasmine, this is my fairy friend, Willow," Trixi introduced them.

Willow stared at their tiaras. "You must be the human girls who've been finding Queen Malice's thunderbolts and solving all the problems they cause!" she exclaimed, her wings fluttering.

Ellie nodded.

Willow grinned. "I'm so glad to meet you. We're all so grateful to you for all your help fighting Queen Malice."

Trixi shook her head sadly. "We think that she's sent a thunderbolt here to Glitter Beach."

"Oh no!" Willow gasped.

"We have to find it before it ruins the ceremony," Ellie added. "Will you help us look?"

"Of course," Willow replied, her wings fluttering anxiously. "I'll ask at the harbor and see if anyone's noticed it."

"We'll check the town," Trixi said.

Willow flew off toward the sea, and the girls and Trixi continued walking to the shops.

"I wish we could be here without

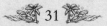

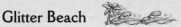

the thunderbolt threatening to ruin everything." Ellie sighed, looking around at the market stalls piled high with beautiful things and the old-fashioned shops with baskets of bright flowers hanging outside. "I'd love to come to Glitter Beach on a vacation!"

Summer and Jasmine agreed. "It is such a pretty place," Summer said. "That's why we can't let Queen Malice wreck it!"

"Let's split up," Jasmine suggested. "We can meet at the clock tower when it strikes eight," she said, pointing at the shimmering silver clock tower in the center of the town square.

"Shout if you spot anything!" Ellie called as she rushed into the nearest shop.

Summer looked around the stalls, where there were fairies selling tiny, polished

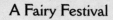

rings made out of wood, and bracelets and clothes stitched from leaves, some green and springlike, and some in the beautiful golden and red colors of autumn.

She talked to a pretty fairy who was selling gorgeous shell boxes and necklaces as well as delicate golden sand castles. But she hadn't seen anything suspicious.

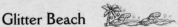

Jasmine walked over to a stall heaped with delicious-looking treats and read the labels: "Icicle snaps, honeydew drops, rose cotton candy." They all looked so yummy that her tummy rumbled loudly! But there was no time to stop and taste them — she had a thunderbolt to find!

As the sound of eight bells rang out across the sea, Trixi and the girls rushed over to the clock tower, shaking their heads as they saw one another.

"There's no sign of trouble anywhere," Trixi sighed.

"There's nothing at the harbor, either," Willow said as she landed next to them.

But just then, Ellie caught sight of something in the sky. "What's that?" she asked. The others followed her gaze. A

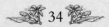

dark cloud seemed to be heading across the water toward Glitter Beach.

"It looks like a tornado!" exclaimed Jasmine.

The cloud coming toward the beach was shaped like a funnel and was swirling around and around. There were cries of alarm as the fairies noticed it, too.

"Quick! It's a whirlwind! Get inside!" Their shouts rang out.

Trixibelle jumped on her leaf and zoomed over to the girls. "Follow me!"

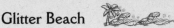

she called, hurrying them inside a shop
behind lots of worried fairies. They
crouched beside a display of tiny acorn
cups and peeked through the window,
looking out to the beach where the
tornado was whirling closer, sweeping
up boats and abandoned mussel-shell
surfboards in its path.

"Look!" Summer cried as the
whirlwind reached the beach and all the
beautiful golden sand started to swirl up
from the ground into it. "It's taking all
the sand!"

The fairies shouted, trying to cast spells
to stop it — but nothing worked.

Just then, Jasmine caught sight of
figures moving in the swirling winds.
"Storm Sprites!" she cried, pointing at the
shadowy shapes.

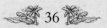

Summer and Ellie gasped as they recognized the nasty creatures that were crouched on clouds moving around and around inside the whirling wind. The sprites screeched with laughter as the tornado whipped around faster and faster. Soon all the sand was gone, and the girls could see that the wind was coming from a jagged black shape in the rocky ground.

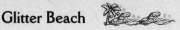

"It's the thunderbolt!" Summer
breathed. It was buried deep in the earth,
with just its black tip showing.

"It must have been under the sand!"
Ellie gasped.

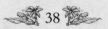

The sprites jeered and laughed as the tornado swept away.

Everyone stared in disbelief. Every single grain of beautiful, sparkling sand had disappeared!

Queen Malice's Mischief

All that was left of the beach was dull rock. Ellie, Jasmine, and Summer ran outside. Trixi and Willow stood next to them, close to tears.

"This is awful!" Trixi cried. "What are we going to do? It's getting dark now, and if the sand's not here when the clock strikes twelve, no one in the kingdom will be able to do any magic for a whole year!"

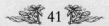

"Don't worry," Ellie said, putting her arm around Trixi. "We'll break the thunderbolt and get the sand back before midnight."

Jasmine nodded. "We've defeated Queen Malice before and we can do it again!"

"There's no way we'll let her get away with this!" Summer vowed.

Trixi looked a little bit happier. "I'd better ask King Merry to come. He'll need to know what his rotten sister has been up to." Trixi tapped her ring and King Merry's name appeared in silvery letters in the air. She tapped her ring a second time and, with a faint popping sound, the words vanished.

"I wonder how long it will take King Merry to arrive," Summer said.

"He'll come as soon as he gets the message," answered Trixi. "He's at the Enchanted Palace at the moment, so he can use the rainbow slide in the garden pond to get anywhere in the kingdom he wants."

"In the meantime, we'd better start figuring this out!" said Jasmine determinedly.

The girls walked around the gray rocky beach, comforting all the fairies they met. Some were crying, others were looking around in horror or pointing at

the thunderbolt. The girls hated seeing them so upset.

Suddenly, a few of the fairies started to point out to sea. The girls followed their gaze. There was a multicolored glimmer in the air over the waves, and where the rainbow met the water, a rather stout person suddenly appeared.

"It's King Merry — and he's on water skis!" gasped Jasmine.

The little round king headed toward them, a water ski on each foot. He was holding onto green seaweed reins, and two dolphins were towing him through the waves. He was wearing long, brightly patterned shorts and yellow water wings, as well as his half-moon glasses. His cloak was blowing in the

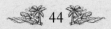

breeze and his crown was perched on
top of a white sun hat.

"Hello, hello!" he
cried as they ran
to the edge
of the water.
Letting go of
the reins with
one hand, he
tried to wave
and lost his
balance. His arms
windmilled wildly.
"Whoa!" he shouted in alarm.

"Oh dear!" Trixi's hand flew to her
mouth as the king toppled backward
into the water. He bobbed around, held
up by his water wings, while the dolphins

circled around him in surprise. "Back in a minute!" Trixi cried as she zoomed over to him on her leaf.

Across the waves the girls saw her tap her pixie ring. The king rose from the water and hovered, the little pixie floating around his shoulders. She pointed to the shore and he began to drift magically across the top of the waves.

"Ah, very good, very good," the girls heard him saying. "Excellent work, Trixi. Hello, girls!" He waved to them again, this time without falling over. Trixi's magic put him gently down on the beach, and Ellie, Summer, and Jasmine rushed over to him. Jasmine was normally the same height as King Merry, but now he loomed over her like a giant! The girls suddenly felt very small. Trixi must have noticed because she tapped her ring and chanted:

"Back to human size you go,
Jasmine, Summer, Ellie — grow!"

The girls shot upward until they were back to normal. Ellie giggled to herself as she realized that King Merry had

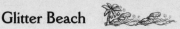

sunglasses on as well as his usual half-moon glasses.

"I came as fast as I could," said the king anxiously. "What has my dreadful sister done now?"

"Her thunderbolt has stolen all the sand from Glitter Beach," Trixi cried. "There's not a single grain left, Your Majesty!"

"Oh, dearie me," King Merry sighed. He looked at the girls. "Have you got a plan to fix it?"

"Not yet," said Jasmine. "The tornado came and whisked the sand away so fast."

"Yes," Ellie added thoughtfully. "But where did it go after that? *Where* did the tornado take the sand?"

"I don't know," said Trixi. "I was too busy looking at the thunderbolt."

"Me too," said Summer.

"Maybe one of the fairies noticed," said Jasmine. "Let's ask around."

"Excellent idea!" King Merry declared.

"Um, maybe first, I might just . . ." Trixi flew around him and tapped her ring. His water wings disappeared in a bright flash.

The king smiled at her and adjusted his crown. "Oh, yes. Thank you, Trixi!"

The fairies were all hovering over the beach, talking anxiously. As King Merry and the girls walked over, they flocked around, talking all at once.

"Oh, please help us!" a little purple-winged fairy cried.

Summer, Ellie, and Jasmine started asking the fairies about the tornado, but no one had seen where it had gone.

"It's no good," said Summer, sitting

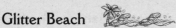
down at last on the rocky beach. The
cloud of fairies fluttered overhead. Ellie and
Jasmine sat down, too, and then Ellie
noticed a familiar-looking fairy flitting
nearby. She looked closely, and realized it
was Willow. She looked so tiny now!

"Hello," Ellie smiled and put out her
hand. The little fairy
landed on it, light as a
feather on her palm.
Willow looked at
them with wide
eyes. "Are you
going to help
us get the
sand back?"

"Yes," Jasmine told
her. "Don't worry,
we'll figure it out."

"But we've got to find out where the tornado went first," said Ellie. "And no one seems to have seen what happened to it."

"I did!" Willow declared.

They all stared at her in amazement.

"I watched it swirl into that cave over there," she continued, pointing to where there were some steep gray cliffs jutting out into the bay. The girls could just see a cave at the base of the cliffs.

"Wonderful!" said Jasmine. "Well
done, Willow!" The little fairy beamed
proudly.

After saying good-bye to Willow, the
girls hurried across the beach.

"Look!" Jasmine hissed as they got
closer to the cave. She pointed ahead.
Even though it was dark, they could just
make out lots of little spiky footprints in
the mud around its entrance.

"Shhh," whispered Ellie. "Listen!"

They could hear high, cackling voices coming from the cave.

"It's the Storm Sprites!" A shiver ran down Ellie's spine as she thought about Queen Malice's spiky-haired helpers.

"What are they doing?" Summer asked shakily.

Jasmine squared her shoulders and looked at them both. "There's only one way to find out. Come on!"

A Cunning Plan

Jasmine, Summer, and Ellie tiptoed up to
the cave entrance. It was a very big cave,
even though they were human-sized now.
As they got closer they could hear the
Storm Sprites shouting at one another.

"Hurry up!" one of them yelled. "Once
Queen Malice has this sand no one will
be able to get in her way anymore!"

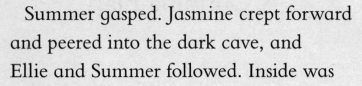

Summer gasped. Jasmine crept forward and peered into the dark cave, and Ellie and Summer followed. Inside was a mountain of glittering golden sand. Eight Storm Sprites were shoveling it into sacks and stacking them up. The girls retreated a little from the cave's entrance. "Willow was right," hissed Ellie. "The sand *is* in the cave!"

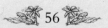

"And the sprites are going to take it to Queen Malice!" said Jasmine. "We've got to stop them!"

They stared at one another, wondering how.

"Yoo-hoo! Girls!" a voice called, making them jump. King Merry was waving as he climbed clumsily over the rocks. Trixi was hovering behind him, holding his cloak up in the air.

"Shhh!' Jasmine hissed, rushing over to the king.

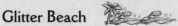

"We've found the sand!" she whispered. "But we've found the Storm Sprites, too!"

Trixi and the king looked very worried as the girls explained what they had seen. "But if they send the sand to Queen Malice, everyone will lose their magic!" King Merry said.

"We need to find a way to get it back," said Jasmine.

Ellie frowned thoughtfully. "Maybe we can sneak in and take the sacks?"

"But the Storm Sprites will see us," Jasmine pointed out.

"The pearl!" Summer exclaimed. "Don't you remember?" she asked as everyone stared at her. "The mermaids gave us a pearl that we could use to turn ourselves invisible!"

There was a bright silver flash and

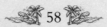

Jasmine gasped as a heavy weight fell into her arms. "The Magic Box!"

She and Ellie glanced at each other in delight. The Magic Box had a wonderful habit of appearing just when it was really needed!

King Merry looked proud. "It really was a very clever invention, wasn't it?" he said to Trixi.

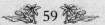

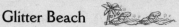

"Exceptionally clever, Your Majesty."
Trixi smiled as the lid of the box slowly
started to open. Tucked inside one of
the little wooden compartments lay a
glowing, shimmering silver pearl.

"We can use this to make ourselves
invisible and get into the cave," Summer
breathed, taking the pearl out of the
box. Almost immediately her fingers and
hands vanished and then suddenly she
disappeared completely!

"Summer? Where have you gone?"
cried Jasmine. Then she jumped as
Summer poked her gently in the ribs.

"I'm still here!" Summer's voice
came from behind them. "Here, hold
my hand."

Jasmine felt Summer's hand touch hers.
She grabbed Ellie's fingers with her other

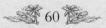

hand. Holding on to one another, all three girls were completely invisible!

"Trixi, what about you?' Jasmine asked from thin air.

"Mermaid magic won't work on the king and me," the pixie said. "I'm afraid you're going to have to do this on your own, girls."

"No problem," Jasmine said bravely. "We'll get the sand back!"

"Hopefully," Summer added rather nervously.

"Of course we will!" Ellie declared.

"Good luck!" Trixi and the king called.

Holding hands, the girls set off to the cave entrance. It was very dark inside, but they could hear the sprites talking to one another and shoveling the sand into the sacks. As their eyes got used to the

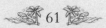

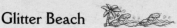

darkness the girls could see the sprites' batlike wings folded against their backs. Ellie, Summer, and Jasmine held their breath as they tiptoed farther into the cave, creeping toward the sand.

Clunk!

Ellie tripped over a spare shovel lying on the ground and it banged noisily against the rocks. The sprites looked up. The girls froze, squeezing one another's hands tightly. A horrible thought crossed Jasmine's mind — the pearl would only keep them invisible for a short while. What if its magic wore off before they got the sand back?

"What was that noise?" asked one sprite.

"I don't know," said another. They looked around suspiciously.

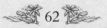

The girls stayed as still as they could. Summer was sure the sprites must be able to hear her heart hammering in her chest.

The sprites slowly got back to work. Jasmine continued to lead the way to the back of the cave but as she did so, she felt a sneeze building in her nose. She swallowed, trying to hold it in, but it was no good . . . all of a sudden it burst out!

"*Ahh-chooo!*"

All the sprites jumped.

"Who's there?" one of them called.

The girls hardly dared to breathe.

"Maybe . . . maybe it's a ghost," said the smallest sprite.

"Don't be a nincompoop," another sprite told him. "There's no such thing as ghosts."

But Ellie saw that all the sprites had started to look slightly worried. *That's it!* she thought, remembering how she had jumped when Molly had leaped out at her back at home. She tugged on Jasmine's hand and whispered as quietly as she could.

"If we pretend to be ghosts we'll scare them so much that they'll run away and we won't have to be invisible! There will be no chance of them coming back again because they'll be too scared!"

Jasmine passed the message on to Summer and then kicked over a nearby sack.

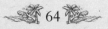

The sprites jumped back in alarm as it fell.

"How did that happen?" one demanded.

"Ghosts!" said the smallest sprite, looking around in alarm. "I told you — it's ghosts!"

Jasmine took a deep breath and started to make a strange howling, moaning noise.

"Argh!" the sprites all yelled. The smallest sprite backed up so quickly he tripped over his shovel and fell to the ground, sending the sprite next to him sprawling. The rest of the sprites started to scramble around as Ellie and then Summer joined in with ghostly noises. Jasmine kicked over two more bags. She was very good at acting and she put on

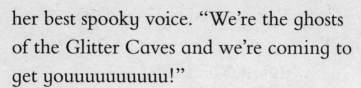

her best spooky voice. "We're the ghosts of the Glitter Caves and we're coming to get youuuuuuuuuu!"

The sprites started to yell and run around. As one ran near them, Ellie had an idea. Using her free hand, she reached out and tickled the sprite.

"Argh! Eee! Argh!" he yelled. "The ghost's got me!"

Ellie had to fight back her giggles. "I am the Tickle Monster Ghost!" she said in a spooky voice like Jasmine, remembering how she had made Molly squeal. "Beware! Bewaaaaaaaaare!" She pulled the others around the cave, poking and prodding at the sprites while Jasmine made spooky noises and Summer pushed the sacks over.

"Forget the silly magic sand!" the smallest sprite shouted. "I'm getting out of here!"

"Me too!" yelled another.

"Me three!" yelped the one on the floor.

All eight sprites charged to the entrance of the cave, pushing and shoving one another as they fled.

"We did it!" Summer said.

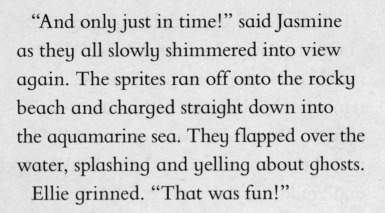

"And only just in time!" said Jasmine as they all slowly shimmered into view again. The sprites ran off onto the rocky beach and charged straight down into the aquamarine sea. They flapped over the water, splashing and yelling about ghosts.

Ellie grinned. "That was fun!"

"And now we can get the sand back to the beach!" said Jasmine.

"Noooooo!" A screech of rage rang through the cave. The girls jumped and swung around. Summer squeaked in alarm and the others caught their breath. There, standing right in the entrance of the cave, was Queen Malice herself!

Stolen Sand

The wicked queen's midnight-dark eyes flashed with fury.

She pointed at the girls with a bony finger. "I have had enough of your meddling, you interfering humans! How dare you keep coming to this land to stop my magic? You will not break my sixth thunderbolt!"

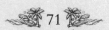

"Malice!" King Merry's voice rang out as he hurried to the cave entrance. "My dear, please stop behaving like this."

"Who are *you* to tell *me* what to do?" hissed Queen Malice.

"He's the king!" Trixi darted around and stopped in the air between him and Queen Malice, her tiny arms folded and a very cross look on her face. "You should listen to him!" she yelled.

The queen glared. "Ha! I won't listen to him, and I certainly won't listen to *you*!" She flicked her fingers and a mini thunderbolt flew from them.

Trixi tried to dodge out of the way, but the thunderbolt caught her leaf and she was thrown through the air.

"Trixi!" the girls gasped as her leaf whirled out of control.

Luckily, Trixi landed in the heap of sand. She sat on the golden grains and pointed her ring at the queen defiantly, but when she tapped it to try to cast a spell, only a few sputtering sparks appeared. "Oh no," Trixi cried unhappily. "My magic is all gone!"

Queen Malice screeched with laughter. "After today no one in the kingdom will have any magic — I'll have it all!" Her voice rose in triumph. "And it will make me more powerful than ever!"

With a clap of her hands, she vanished — taking all the sand with her!

Ellie, Jasmine, and Summer stared in horror. "Now what are we going to do?" exclaimed Jasmine.

With the pile of sand gone, Trixi was left sitting on the cave floor, her leaf beside her. She burst into tears.

"She's right. Without the sand there won't be any magic for the whole year."

Summer couldn't bear seeing Trixi so upset. She picked her up gently. "Please don't worry. There's still time for us to solve the problem."

"Not much, I'm afraid." King Merry pointed outside. Night had fallen while the girls had been in the cave, and Glitter Beach was bathed in moonlight. "It's almost midnight."

Trixi started to sob even more loudly.

The girls went to the entrance. Down on the beach the fairies were fluttering around like they were lost. The jagged black edges of the thunderbolt stuck up out of the rocks, casting shadows as spiky as Queen Malice's crown.

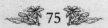

"There must be a way to fix things," said Jasmine, pacing up and down.

"Usually, to break the thunderbolt, we need to reverse the magic," Summer said thoughtfully. "This thunderbolt has stolen the sand. If we can put it back on the beach, then maybe the spell will be broken."

"But we don't have any sand," Ellie pointed out. "Queen Malice has taken it all."

"Not all of it!" Summer gasped. "Look!" She pointed at Trixi. The little pixie's hair and clothes were still coated with fine grains of shimmering sand from when she had been knocked into the pile by Queen Malice.

"But is that enough sand to break the spell?" Ellie said.

"There's only one way to find out!" cried Jasmine.

With Summer carrying Trixi carefully in her hands, they all ran outside.

Summer had just stepped out of the cave when a bony leg poked out in front of her and she tripped.

"Argh!" she cried, letting go of Trixi as she put her hands out to stop herself from falling.

Trixi managed to catch hold of her leaf and jump on before she crashed to the ground, but as she did so a few of the tiny grains of sand on her clothes fell off. "The sand!" she cried.

An evil laugh came from behind her. A Storm Sprite was flapping toward her, reaching out his bony fingers to grab her.

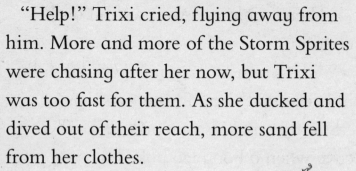

"Help!" Trixi cried, flying away from him. More and more of the Storm Sprites were chasing after her now, but Trixi was too fast for them. As she ducked and dived out of their reach, more sand fell from her clothes.

King Merry, Summer, Ellie, and Jasmine stared up in dismay. "What can we do?" King Merry asked. The girls looked at one another helplessly.

Ellie tried jumping and catching a Storm Sprite as he passed overhead, but he was flying too high. "If only we could fly!" she said in frustration.

"I know some fairies who can!" Jasmine shouted, running off toward the beach.

"We have to try and catch some of the sand," Ellie told Summer. The girls ran underneath Trixi as she zoomed around overhead, holding their hands up to catch the falling grains. King Merry held his cloak out and tried to catch some, too.

"It's impossible!" Ellie cried as more of the precious sand fell off Trixi's clothes and was lost in a rock pool below.

Suddenly there was a shout and Jasmine came running back toward the cave, looking quite out of breath. Above her fluttered a cloud of furious fairies.

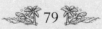

"Go away, you horrid sprites!" one shouted.

"How dare you steal our sand!"

The fairies flew around the Storm Sprites, keeping just out of reach of their pointy fingers. There were so many fairies that the sprites couldn't see if Trixi was among them. "There she is!" one of the sprites yelled.

"No, she's over here!" another shouted.

The girls looked up. Even they couldn't tell if Trixi was hidden in the whirling mass of fairies!

"Psst!" came a tiny voice from below them. "I'm down here!" Trixi was on the ground, hiding behind a rock.

Jasmine, Summer, Ellie, and King Merry crept over to her. The little pixie looked very sad. "I lost all the sand," she cried. "Did you catch any?"

They all checked their hands and clothes, but there was no sand anywhere.

Trixi sighed and her shoulders dropped. She turned to look at the beach. "The sand is supposed to be so beautiful, glinting in the moonlight," she said sadly. "I wish we could have seen it."

"I can!" Summer gasped. She pointed

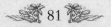

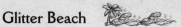

at King Merry's purple cloak. There, twinkling like a golden star, was a single grain of sand!

"Oh, well done, King Merry!" the girls shouted.

"Hold still, King Merry," Jasmine said, carefully reaching toward the precious grain of sand with her nimble fingers.

Summer let out a breath as Jasmine picked it up. "Quickly! We have to put it on the beach before the clock strikes midnight!"

Running as fast as they could, the girls rushed down to where the sea glinted in the moonlight.

"Here goes!" cried Jasmine, delicately placing the glimmering grain onto the rocky shore.

The girls held hands as the sand

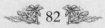

touched the gray rocks. For a second,
nothing happened. Then, with a massive
crack, the thunderbolt on the beach
shattered into black fragments.

Ellie felt something falling on her. It felt
like the finest, lightest rain. Looking up,
she gasped. "It's raining sand!"

Sand floated down from the sky, shining
in the moonlight and tickling the girls'
skin. All around them, the fairies noticed
and started to cheer.

"It worked!" cried Trixi as the fairies
started to dance and fly, swooping and
swirling in the glittering air.

"We did it," gasped Ellie, hugging the
others. "We've broken the spell and
the sand's back — and just in time!"

King Merry threw his crown into the
air in joy. "We've saved the day — I

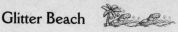

mean, the night — and we've destroyed my sister's last thunderbolt!" He began to dance a jig.

Jasmine grabbed the others' hands and pulled them around in a circle. The sand felt soft beneath their feet and they swirled faster and faster, shrieking in delight. The girls saw Willow and Trixi dancing together nearby in the sky. They waved and the two friends waved back. All around them, fairies fluttered excitedly, laughing and shouting for joy.

Trixi swooped down to the girls. "It's nearly midnight!" she cried excitedly. "The midsummer magic is about to start!"

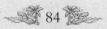

Midsummer Magic

The sand on the beach began to sparkle
and glow as if it was made of lots
of tiny jewels. The shimmer spread
from the beach out into the sea, and even
the air seemed to glitter with light. The
fairies called out in delight as the glow
surrounded them, making them twinkle
from their toes to the tips of their wings.

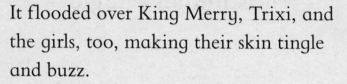

It flooded over King Merry, Trixi, and the girls, too, making their skin tingle and buzz.

"Glitter dust," King Merry said with a sigh of contentment. "The magic is working!"

With a delighted smile, he sat down on some nearby rocks.

"Look how happy everyone is," murmured Ellie as two fairies fluttered past, twirling and looping in the air as the clock rang out twelve times.

On the final chime, there was a bright silver flash and then the sparkling sand became a soft shimmering gold again.

"We've all got our magic back for another year, thanks to you," Trixi cried, whizzing up to the girls. "And on Midsummer's Eve, you don't even need

a magic spell or a
pixie ring. Look!"
She pointed in
front of her.
"Shining star!"
she declared.
A star popped
into the air. It
floated toward the
pixie, glittering like a
diamond, and landed in her hand.

Ellie remembered what Trixi had said
earlier. "Will we have absorbed any
magic?"

"I don't know," Trixi laughed. "Try
doing some!"

Summer held out her hand rather
cautiously. "Um, a flower!" she said.
There was a bright flash and a gorgeous

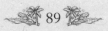

golden flower sprang out of the sand!
Giggling in delight, Summer bent down
and picked it. It smelled amazing!

Ellie couldn't resist. "I'd like a drawing
set!" She pointed in front of her and a
sketchbook appeared, along with a gold
box containing pencils in every possible
color. They floated toward Ellie, the
sketchbook opening as if inviting her
to draw. She chose a pencil and began to
sketch Trixi. When she finished, there
was a shimmer and the drawing started
to move on the page, waving at her, just
like the real pixie. "This is amazing!"
cried Ellie.

"My turn!" said Jasmine excitedly. "I'd
love a guitar!" she called, pointing in
front of her. Instantly, there was a guitar
in the air in front of her. Its strings were

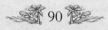

made of shining gold and it was studded
with bright pink gems. Jasmine whooped
and grabbed it, strumming the strings
happily. She remembered the song she had
once played for the king's birthday and
began to play it now, changing a few lines:

The Secret Kingdom is a magical place,
Even the moon has a smiley face.
Midsummer's Eve is a time of fun,
Now that Malice's meanness
is undone.

As Jasmine's song filled the air, the
fairies joined in, and even King Merry
whistled with them. Ellie sang along,
drawing everything that was happening.
Summer made garlands of flowers for
everyone.

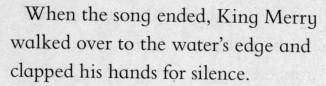

When the song ended, King Merry walked over to the water's edge and clapped his hands for silence.

"Once again, my sister's wicked plans have been stopped by our three human friends," he proclaimed proudly. "All six thunderbolts have now been found, their magic spells have been broken, and the danger to our wonderful Secret Kingdom has passed."

A worrying thought crossed Ellie's mind. It was wonderful that they had stopped Queen Malice, but now that all six thunderbolts had been found, would she, Summer, and Jasmine be needed in the Secret Kingdom again? An icy chill ran over her skin. Maybe this was their last visit.

"No," she whispered.

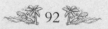

"What is it?" Summer said, seeing her face.

But before Ellie could explain, the king was talking again. "To show my gratitude for all they have done, I have a gift for Summer, Ellie, and Jasmine." He patted a silver box on the table next to him. "My dears, would you come up?"

Everyone cheered as the girls walked onto the stage. He handed them a bag made of glittering silver material. On the front of it was a small embroidered crescent — the same shape as the island.

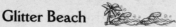

"There is glitter dust in this bag," the king explained as the girls thanked him. "If you need to, you can use it to cast a spell. But use it wisely. There is only enough for one spell each."

Jasmine's fingers tightened on the little pouch as she realized that this gift would fill the final empty compartment in the Magic Box. It was an amazing present, but Jasmine felt like she was about to cry. Did this mean they wouldn't have any more magical adventures? She looked at Summer, whose lip was trembling, and knew she was thinking the same thing.

"King Merry, is this the last time we'll get to visit the Secret Kingdom?" Jasmine burst out.

As the king opened his mouth to reply there was a noise from the sea and a

small black boat came flying over the waves.

"It's Queen Malice!" gasped Trixi as the fairies shrieked and cried out.

Two fierce sea serpents pulled the queen's black boat. She stood in the bow, holding long reins and cracking a whip. In the back of her boat crouched the Storm Sprites, jeering and cackling.

Queen Malice pulled the reins and, with a spray of seawater, the serpents stopped. "You think you've defeated me, you pesky brats," she cried. "But I'll be back! Here's a little something for you to remember me by!" She clapped her hands and a thunderbolt shot straight toward the beach!

"We have to stop it!" Summer cried. "Can we use magic?"

"Trixi's pixie magic never works against Queen Malice's spells," Summer said anxiously.

"But our magic is extra strong tonight because we've just absorbed so much glitter dust," Trixi said. "If all the fairies worked together . . ."

"And us, we've got magic, too!" Ellie exclaimed.

"It might just work!" Trixi said. She flew high overhead and shouted as loud as she could:

*"Fairy friends, this midsummer's night,
Malice's magic we can fight!"*

She pointed her hands at the thunderbolt and in an instant every fairy was doing the same. Ellie, Jasmine, and Summer copied them, and wished as hard as they could that the thunderbolt would break. Suddenly, silvery blue light shot out from their hands.

"It's working!" Summer cried.

The thunderbolt hit the wall of light and shattered into a million pieces that flew toward Queen Malice.

"Nooooooo!" she screeched, diving into

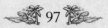

the water as the shards hit her boat, which broke and started to sink. The Storm Sprites climbed onto one of the sea serpents and helped a soggy Queen Malice onto another. "You haven't seen the last of me!" she shouted as the serpent carried her away. "Just you wait and see!"

Everyone stared after Queen Malice in amazement.

"You asked me whether you will come back," King Merry said softly, as Trixi hovered beside his ear, looking serious. "Well, I have a strong feeling that we will need your help again very soon."

Ellie, Jasmine, and Summer looked at one another and smiled.

"We'll come whenever you need us," Jasmine promised. Ellie and Summer nodded.

The fairies all cheered. The air filled with relieved chatter and tinkly fairy laughter.

Jasmine, Ellie, and Summer hugged one another. Trixi and the fairies linked hands and flew around them in a glittering circle.

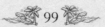

"The Secret Kingdom is safe for now," Summer said, smiling.

"We'll be back again soon," Ellie added.

"And we'll fight whatever Queen Malice throws at us!" Jasmine said.

As they celebrated, Summer's flower garlands faded away. The guitar and sketchbook vanished, too, and the girls gave a happy sigh. Their magic had lasted just long enough!

King Merry clapped his hands. "The time has come to say farewell to our human friends — for now." He turned to the girls. "Thank you, from the bottom of all our hearts."

Trixi flew over to them, tears in her blue eyes. "I'll miss all of you so much!" She kissed each of them on the nose. "I've loved the adventures we've had together."

"We'll miss you, too," Ellie told her, feeling her own eyes prickle.

"See you soon!" called Trixi.

Jasmine, Ellie, and Summer waved to all their Secret Kingdom friends, then joined hands. Trixi tapped her ring and a sparkly whirlwind started to swirl around the girls.

All around them they could hear fairy voices ringing out to bid them farewell.

"Good-bye!" the girls called as they were scooped up into the air and whisked away.

They landed safely back in Ellie's bedroom. For a moment, they all blinked. "We're home," Ellie said, looking around sadly.

"The box, too," said Summer in relief, looking down at the Magic Box, which was now sitting safely on the rug in front of them.

The lid glowed and opened and the girls placed their precious bag of glitter dust inside.

"We've had some amazing adventures," said Jasmine as the box slowly shut.

"We will go back, won't we?" Summer asked anxiously.

"Look!" said Ellie as a ripple of light crossed the mirrored top. They all peered eagerly into the shining surface. "It's King Merry and Trixi!" she exclaimed.

The king's kindly face beamed out at them while Trixi hovered beside him on her leaf. Words slowly floated up and formed in the mirror:

Thank you, Ellie, Summer, and Jasmine.
We will see you again soon!

The girls grinned and waved back in delight. With a flicker, the image slowly faded and the box returned to normal.

"Yes, we'll go back," Ellie said, feeling certain.

"And we'll see all our friends again," said Summer.

"And have new adventures!" said Jasmine, her eyes shining.

The three girls smiled at one another. The Secret Kingdom was waiting for them. One day the Magic Box would glow again — and they could hardly wait!

Find out how their Secret Kingdom
adventure began when Ellie,
Summer, and Jasmine visit the

Enchanted Palace

A Mysterious Find

"I think I'm finished now, ma'am. Where
would you like this box to go?" Summer
Hammond asked as she packed up the
last two books from her station.

"I'm finished here, too," Jasmine Smith
added, putting the last things into a box.

Mrs. Benson smiled. "Goodness! That
was fast work, girls. Well done."

Ellie Macdonald poked her head up from behind a table, tucking a wiry red curl behind her ear. "Hey, nobody told me it was a race!" Laughter danced in her green eyes as she stood up.

Jasmine winked at Summer. "It looks like we're the champions!"

"You're all champions," Mrs. Benson said as she smiled at the three girls. "This was the school's most successful rummage sale ever, and it was all thanks to you!"

Although they were all very different from one another, Ellie, Summer, and Jasmine were as close as sisters. They all lived in the same town and had been best friends since they first started elementary school.

Summer was shy, and tugged at her blond braids whenever she felt nervous.

She often had her head buried in a book, either reading about the natural world or writing poems and stories about her animal friends.

Jasmine was outgoing and always in a hurry, with her long dark hair whipping around her as she raced from one thing to another. She loved singing and dancing and being in the spotlight.

Ellie was a joker, and was always the first to laugh at her own clumsiness. She was also very artistic and loved drawing. Together the girls made quite a team!

"It was nothing really," Summer said, blushing at their teacher's praise. "The books I sold were mostly my old ones from our attic."

"Well, they were very popular," said Mrs. Benson. "And, Jasmine, you played that guitar wonderfully. After everyone heard you, we sold it in no time."

Jasmine grinned. "No problem, Mrs. Benson. You know I love music!"

"And the fashion boutique was a great success, too — especially those superb Ellie Macdonald designs!" Mrs. Benson picked up a T-shirt with a bold green-and-purple pattern on it. She looked over at Ellie. "Thanks so much for making one for me."

"Do you like the design?" Ellie said. "Green and purple are my favorite colors."

"You don't say!" Jasmine's hazel eyes twinkled with amusement as she looked at her friend's flowery purple-and-green dress, her green leggings, and her purple ballet flats!

Ellie chuckled, then turned to pick up her bag. But as she did, she tripped over something and fell to the floor with a *thump*.

"Ouch!"

"Are you okay?" asked Mrs. Benson.

"I'm fine — it's just my two left feet, as usual!" Ellie said as she stood up. "But what's this?"

She picked up the object she'd tripped over — an old wooden box. It was as large as her outstretched hand and made out of solid wood with a curved lid. The whole thing was thick with dust, but under the grime Ellie could tell the box was beautiful. Its sides were carved with intricate patterns that she couldn't quite make out, and on the lid was a mirror, surrounded by six glass stones. Ellie wiped the lid with her sleeve and could just see her reflection. As she held the box, light swirled in the stones. It looked almost . . . magical. "How strange," she murmured. "I'm sure it wasn't here a minute ago."

Jasmine took the box and tried to open it. "The lid's stuck down," she said. "It won't budge."

Mrs. Benson glanced at her watch. "Well, wherever it came from, it's too late to sell it now. Why don't you girls take it home — you never know, you might find a way to open it."

Read

Enchanted Palace

to see how it
all began!

Be in on the secret.
Collect them all!

Enjoy six sparkling adventures.
www.secretkingdombooks.com

Character Profile:
King Merry

Personality:
Kind and clever, but sometimes confused. Luckily, Trixi's usually around to look after him!

Favorite place in the Secret Kingdom:
His special snuggly throne in his Enchanted Palace.

Guide the Girls

Oh no! The awful Storm Sprites have
trapped Trixibelle in the Glitter Beach caves! Can you
guide Ellie, Jasmine, and Summer and help them find her?

Ellie, Summer,
and Jasmine

should take
path

_____

A   B   C

RAINBOW magic™

Which Magical Fairies Have You Met?

- ❏ The Rainbow Fairies
- ❏ The Weather Fairies
- ❏ The Jewel Fairies
- ❏ The Pet Fairies
- ❏ The Dance Fairies
- ❏ The Music Fairies
- ❏ The Sports Fairies
- ❏ The Party Fairies
- ❏ The Ocean Fairies
- ❏ The Night Fairies
- ❏ The Magical Animal Fairies
- ❏ The Princess Fairies
- ❏ The Superstar Fairies
- ❏ The Fashion Fairies
- ❏ The Sugar & Spice Fairies
- ❏ The Earth Fairies
- ❏ The Magical Crafts Fairies

▌SCHOLASTIC

Find all of your favorite fairy friends at
scholastic.com/rainbowmagic

HIT entertainment

RMFAIRY11

RAINBOW magic™

SPECIAL EDITION

Which Magical Fairies Have You Met?

3 stories in each one!

- ☐ Joy the Summer Vacation Fairy
- ☐ Holly the Christmas Fairy
- ☐ Kylie the Carnival Fairy
- ☐ Stella the Star Fairy
- ☐ Shannon the Ocean Fairy
- ☐ Trixie the Halloween Fairy
- ☐ Gabriella the Snow Kingdom Fairy
- ☐ Juliet the Valentine Fairy
- ☐ Mia the Bridesmaid Fairy
- ☐ Flora the Dress-Up Fairy
- ☐ Paige the Christmas Play Fairy
- ☐ Emma the Easter Fairy
- ☐ Cara the Camp Fairy
- ☐ Destiny the Rock Star Fairy
- ☐ Belle the Birthday Fairy
- ☐ Olympia the Games Fairy
- ☐ Selena the Sleepover Fairy
- ☐ Cheryl the Christmas Tree Fairy
- ☐ Florence the Friendship Fairy
- ☐ Lindsay the Luck Fairy
- ☐ Brianna the Tooth Fairy
- ☐ Autumn the Falling Leaves Fairy
- ☐ Keira the Movie Star Fairy
- ☐ Addison the April Fool's Day Fairy
- ☐ Bailey the Babysitter Fairy
- ☐ Natalie the Christmas Stocking Fairy
- ☐ Lila and Myla the Twins Fairies

■ SCHOLASTIC

Find all of your favorite fairy friends at
scholastic.com/rainbowmagic

HIT entertainment

RMSPECIAL14

The Rescue Princesses

These are no ordinary princesses—
they're Rescue Princesses!